Acting Edition

I0741576

~~Business ideas??~~
~~Bu$ine$$ Idea$~~
~~Biz nas Ideaz~~
BUSINESS IDEAS

by Milo Cramer

SAMUEL FRENCH

ISBN 978-0-573-71197-8

www.concordtheatricals.com
www.concordtheatricals.co.uk

FOR PRODUCTION INQUIRIES

UNITED STATES AND CANADA
info@concordtheatricals.com
1-866-979-0447

UNITED KINGDOM AND EUROPE
licensing@concordtheatricals.co.uk
020-7054-7298

Each title is subject to availability from Concord Theatricals Corp.,
depending upon country of performance. Please be aware that
BUSINESS IDEAS may not be licensed by Concord Theatricals Corp.
in your territory. Professional and amateur producers should contact
the nearest Concord Theatricals Corp. office or licensing partner to
verify availability.

No one shall make any changes in this title(s) for the purpose of production. No part of this book may be reproduced, stored in a retrieval system, scanned, uploaded, or transmitted in any form, by any means, now known or yet to be invented, including mechanical, electronic, digital, photocopying, recording, videotaping, or otherwise, without the prior written permission of the publisher. No one shall share this title(s), or any part of this title(s), through any social media or file hosting websites.

For all inquiries regarding motion picture, television, online/digital and other media rights, please contact Concord Theatricals Corp.

MUSIC AND THIRD-PARTY MATERIALS USE NOTE

Licensees are solely responsible for obtaining formal written permission from copyright owners to use copyrighted music and/or other copyrighted third-party materials (e.g. artworks, logos) in the performance of this play and are strongly cautioned to do so. If no such permission is obtained by the licensee, then the licensee must use only original music and materials that the licensee owns and controls. Licensees are solely responsible and liable for clearances of all third-party copyrighted materials, including without limitation music, and shall indemnify the copyright owners of the play(s) and their licensing agent, Concord Theatricals Corp., against any costs, expenses, losses and liabilities arising from the use of such copyrighted third-party materials by licensees. For music, please contact the appropriate music licensing authority in your territory for the rights to any incidental music.

IMPORTANT BILLING AND CREDIT REQUIREMENTS

If you have obtained performance rights to this title, please refer to your licensing agreement for important billing and credit requirements.

BUSINESS IDEAS was first produced by The Alliance Theater in Atlanta, GA, in November 2024. The performance was directed by Matt Torney, with sets by Chika Shimizu, costumes by April Andrew Carswell, lights by Alberto Segarra, sound by Jimmy Garver, and stage management by Rodney Williams. The cast was as follows:

LISA . . . . Devon Hales
GEORGINA . . . . Courtenay Collins
PATTY . . . . Michelle Pokopac
CUSTOMERS . . . . Courtney Patterson

BUSINESS IDEAS was subsequently produced by Clubbed Thumb in New York City in June 2025. The performance was directed by Laura Dupper, with sets by Emmie Finckel, costumes by Avery Reed, lights by Emily Clarkson, sound by Caroline Eng, and stage management by Andie Burns. The cast was as follows:

LISA . . . . Laura Scott Carey
GEORGINA . . . . Annie McNamara
PATTY . . . . Brittany Bradford
CUSTOMERS . . . . Mary Wiseman

BUSINESS IDEAS was developed through the Mabou Mines Resident Artist Program and Clubbed Thumb's directing fellowship, directed by Andrés Lopez-Alicea. It was further supported by Cygnet Theater's Finish Line Commission and the University of California, San Diego.

CHARACTERS

LISA – a teenager
GEORGINA – her mom
PATTY – their server
CUSTOMERS – all played by one actor

SETTING

a café.
a cute café where you can work on your MacBook ;)
lots of coffee kitsch? i.e.:

    SIP HAPPENS
    STRESSED, BLESSED, AND COFFEE OBSESSED
    HOT STUFF

AUTHOR'S NOTES

There are multiple ways the casting of these four roles can break down racially, each with different connotations – I hope casting choices are made collaboratively wherever the play is performed.

Some of the customers are men, but none of the actors are. Lisa and/or Patty might be nonbinary; Georgina wouldn't know what that means.

Props should be either functional or emotional – tiny sugar packets, an old mop, Post-It notes. There is no need for literal coffee equipment.

Love and gratitude to my family.

1. Slowww Customer

*(**SLOWWW CUSTOMER** is kind of a bro. **PATTY** at work behind the counter. Six a.m.)*

SLOWWW CUSTOMER. *(Molasses.)* ...do I order here? or

PATTY. order?

SLOWWW CUSTOMER. ...huh?

PATTY. do you "order"?

or do you ask politely

SLOWWW CUSTOMER. okay, what do I *want*. hmmmmm

(Pause.)

PATTY. is it o/kay if I –

SLOWWW CUSTOMER. *(Hey crazy question:)* what do you like?

PATTY. ...coffee.

SLOWWW CUSTOMER. yeah but coffee's not really my *thing* hey. haha.

you're funny. "coffee."

hey, how's your day going?

PATTY. fine.

SLOWWW CUSTOMER. yeah well mine's a piece of shit.

OK, what do I *want*.

Hmmmmmmmmmm

(Pause.)

PATTY. can I go do something else?

SLOWWW CUSTOMER. huh?

PATTY. can I go do something else while you make up your mind?

SLOWWW CUSTOMER. aren't you here all day?

like "haha I'm here all day"

like that's what they usually say?

like "haha I'm not going anywhere"

PATTY. I just want to walk five feet that way

SLOWWW CUSTOMER. *(Genuinely confused –)* but I'm a customer

(Long pause.)

PATTY. can I ask you a question?

SLOWWW CUSTOMER. *(A revelation! Miraculous.)* Tea! I'll have "tea."

PATTY. what do you *do*?

SLOWWW CUSTOMER. I try not to do anything, ha.

PATTY. but like

what's your job?

SLOWWW CUSTOMER. *(Like a TED Talk.)* why is everyone so obsessed with work?

who cares what I "do"?

could any question be more boring?

ask me something real, I dare you.

ask me what I love.

PATTY. *(Retreating, mechanical, putting up a wall, dead inside.)* nevermind that'll be five seventy-five we're cashless we don't take cash feel free to tip or not tip totally up to you milks are on the side bathroom code is 1111 thanks so much have a good one.

SLOWWW CUSTOMER. *(Ashamed.)* if you must know

...

I'm a kindergarten teacher

2. Mother Daughter Team

(**LISA**, *half-asleep, miserable, stands where*
SLOWWW CUSTOMER *stood –)*

LISA. *(The first of many echoes.)* do we –

order here? or

PATTY. order?

LISA. huh

PATTY. do you "order"?

or do you ask politely

(**GEORGINA** *arrives like a bullet train or like
a sneaky spy –)*

GEORGINA. I think we just…take a seat

LISA. we haven't ordered anything?

GEORGINA. shhh it's kinda fun, it's like a heist

LISA. we'll get kicked out –

GEORGINA. I brought supplies.

LISA. we're in public (?)

(**GEORGINA** *starts setting up –)*

GEORGINA. The time has come. For you and me. To start
a business.

LISA. it's 6 a.m.

GEORGINA. this is the kinda place people Start Businesses.

LISA. …this place?

GEORGINA. "Cool" it's "Cool"

LISA. a "Business"?

GEORGINA. a business, you know, like –

Ford Motor Company

Etsy

LISA. we're not gonna start – Etsy –

GEORGINA. never say never

LISA. *(Nice voice, letting her down gently, confident this will work:)* Mom?

hate to break it to you but –

I heard you have to be Already Rich to start a business?

GEORGINA. don't be silly. anyone can start a business.

LISA. can they?

GEORGINA. duh. that's the whole point.

of businesses. of America!

LISA. um,

GEORGINA. seed funding, we'll get seed funding.

LISA. from who?

GEORGINA. *(Worst possible tactic.)* also, honey, also – this is a good opportunity – for us to bond :)

> *(**LISA** groans.)*
>
> *(A sleepy stubborn angry groan.)*
>
> *(She curls up into a little ball? It goes on too long?)*

LISA. uuugguggggggggghghghghghghghghghghghghghgh hhhhhhhhhh.

> *(Maybe somewhere in the middle of that, or afterwards, **GEORGINA** starts this little chant:)*

GEORGINA. Mother Daughter Team.

Mother Daughter Team.

How sexy is that?

(Beat.)

do you wanna go to college or not.

LISA. I didn't know

that was like

in question.

...

is that in question?

3. Anxious Customer

(**ANXIOUS CUSTOMER** *gets too close? Never leaves home? Is a hoarder.)*

ANXIOUS CUSTOMER. you forgot to Stamp me?

PATTY. ..."stamp" you?

ANXIOUS CUSTOMER. Stamp me!

...Stamp me, Stamp my Stamp card?

I got two coffees, you owe me two coffee Stamps.

PATTY. so,

company policy is No Free Stamps.

ANXIOUS CUSTOMER. free? haha. no.

you *owe me* Stamps.

PATTY. company policy –

ANXIOUS CUSTOMER. it costs you nothing.

it costs you nothing to Stamp my Stamp card

PATTY. I'll get in trouble

ANXIOUS CUSTOMER. are you a child? are-you-a-robot?

PATTY. I'm an employee

ANXIOUS CUSTOMER. I'm a human person.

you have the opportunity to do something nice.

PATTY. why is this impor/tant to you (?)

ANXIOUS CUSTOMER. it's just frustrating because I have twenty half-full Stamp cards at home, I keep losing them.

I don't know what's wrong with me.

PATTY. I've never seen you before

ANXIOUS CUSTOMER. are you new here?

> *(Pause.)*

are you new here? because

this is kind of my local spot

PATTY. *(Very delicately?)* I've worked here. for five years.

ANXIOUS CUSTOMER. are you like the weekend girl?

> *(Pause! Pain.)*

PATTY. no. I am not like the "weekend" "girl"

I am like the six days a week, ten hours a day, nine dollars an hour plus tips

...adult.

ANXIOUS CUSTOMER. it's not like a real adult job-job, though, is it?

PATTY. well what do you do, freak?

because I'm actually –

> *(Catching herself, switching from angry to network-y.)*

seeking other employment

ANXIOUS CUSTOMER. I'm a therapist

4. Crepe (Crape?) Cart

GEORGINA. you – are gonna to look so cute –

in a little yellow apron –

with a little yellow umbrella –

manning our very own crepe cart

downtown!

we could even just do weekends

LISA. ...first we need to figure out if it's pronounced "crepe" or "crape"

GEORGINA. crepe

LISA. crape, no / crape

GEORGINA. crepe.

creee–

GEORGINA.	**LISA**.
–ep	–ape
–ep	
	crap

GEORGINA. but I have a French friend a real French friend who says crepe

LISA. google says crape

GEORGINA. but crepe *sounds* better

LISA. you think I want to stand

at some heavy ass cart

and pour, what, *batter*?

for asshole strangers? for ten hours?

GEORGINA. everyone's gonna have a crush on you.

LISA. while you do what.

GEORGINA. Strategy.

Image management.

LISA. sitting in air conditioning –

GEORGINA. from each according to her ability,

to each according to her need.

LISA. but I wanna do something cool

GEORGINA. you're just afraid of hard work

of accepting a position that compromises your entitlement

but newsflash –

(**LISA** *isn't paying attention.*)

LISA. mom sorry I can't pay attention when you talk about this business stuff like at all.

like one major class barrier I can identify right now...

is just how boring this stuff is

5. Apologizing Customer

APOLOGIZING CUSTOMER. sorry, so so sorry,

but could you please pour just a *little* more cashew milk? into my coffee?

stupid, it's stupid, I know.

I promise I could not be more ashamed of myself.

> *(But* **PATTY** *is lost in an inner reverie – Prince Hamlet:)*

PATTY. O, me

Why must I have experiences?

Why must I feel so acutely what befalls

These, my fingers

This, my heart

Yet not at all what happens to

Yon table?

Yonder tree?

Why do I stop where I stop?

How strange that matter has arranged itself into me, this fleshy vessel

How strange that matter has arranged itself...at all

> *(The cashew milk is overflowing.)*

APOLOGIZING CUSTOMER. ahhh not too much milk! ahhh not too too much!

PATTY. ...just right, right?

APOLOGIZING CUSTOMER. please just like a *light* nutty chocolate color

PATTY. I really want.

to make it perfect for you.

APOLOGIZING CUSTOMER. god you must hate me.

you must want to kill me.

I just was really looking forward to this coffee!

and in my mind I'm weighing like:

is it worth annoying the cool girl...?

to get the perfect coffee...? maybe not...?

but then it's like: I paid four dollars...?

PATTY. there is no way to be a good customer.

accept you are a bad customer without bitterness and move on.

APOLOGIZING CUSTOMER. I need you to like me in order to feel good about myself

I wish I could buy coffee without having a crisis!

Ordering is the first thing you learn in any language.

PATTY. what about, like, "ma-ma"?

or "hi"?

APOLOGIZING CUSTOMER. could you actually please maybe

go pour a little milk *out*?

>   *(Halt.)*

>   *(**PATTY** glowers.)*

PATTY. what do you do?

APOLOGIZING CUSTOMER. ugh, what don't I do

PATTY. I'm just trying to figure out, like.

what jobs...*are* there

APOLOGIZING CUSTOMER.   I'm an administrative
assistant it's so awful I don't even wanna think about it.

...coming here is the best part of my day

6. Little Books By The Cash Register

GEORGINA. *(Pitching.)* Little Books by the Cash Register.

　　　(Beat.)

LISA. little books...by which cash register?

GEORGINA. The. The.

LISA. that's the name of our company?

GEORGINA. just any little book that goes by the cash register that you think "I want to buy it"

LISA. but what's one entry like Name One

GEORGINA. *(Whispering?)* it makes me furious *other* people are out there doing little books

when *we* could be the ones doing them.

LISA. I dunno "little books" will pay my tuition –

GEORGINA. watch, just you watch.

LISA. who's the target audience?

GEORGINA. shoppers!

LISA. who?

GEORGINA. You're by a cash register. You're sad.

Your life lacks whimsy.

And what should be smiling up at you

But a little book!

About anything. France.

Designed by a *mother-daughter team.*

LISA. people don't read.

people hate reading.

GEORGINA. ! maybe it's not books, maybe it's anything.

little anything by the cash register.

LISA. *(Dry.)* little anything anywhere

GEORGINA. are you trying to hurt my feelings?

LISA. people shop online.

no one is "by" cash registers anymore.

GEORGINA. I don't care.

I want to do this.

I have to.

LISA. also, just, mom?

nobody cares about stupid shit

> *(Low, cool –)*

> *(Thinks this will get her daughter interested –)*

GEORGINA. Hey.

We could do a gay book.

LISA. *wow*

GEORGINA. people like buying gay things.

and feminist things.

LISA. I'm leaving.

GEORGINA. what? they do.

LISA. you're breaking my heart right now.

GEORGINA. gay...book

gay...pages in the book

LISA. no.

GEORGINA. please?

LISA. no.

GEORGINA. *(Excited.)* ooooooo –

or *poor man's series*

LISA. *(Dread.)* what's a poor man's series?

GEORGINA. It's a market that hasn't been tapped.

It's an *identity*

that hasn't been *co-opted*

LISA. is "poor" an identity?

GEORGINA. and it's authentic,

it's authentic because we're poor

LISA. we have a washer-dryer

GEORGINA. poor man's something is a something.

LISA. I don't understand

GEORGINA. help me out here

poor man's poem is a sentence.

LISA. that's a business?

GEORGINA. Poor man's dictionary?

Poor Man's Cookbook!

LISA. what do poor men cook?

GEORGINA. *Poor Man's Cookbook*, COLON –

This is good.

Poor Man's Cookbook, Colon – Colon –

Colon what?

7. Curious Customer

(**CURIOUS CUSTOMER** *is femme, inquisitive, chewing gum –*)

CURIOUS CUSTOMER. large coffffffffffrrrr –

wait a minute.

don't I know you?

PATTY. no.

CURIOUS CUSTOMER. ...I know you!

I do know you!

PATTY. nope

CURIOUS CUSTOMER. I know you from somewhere.

I knowwwwww you.

PATTY. we don't know each other.

CURIOUS CUSTOMER. who ARE YOU?

PATTY. that's the question, alright

CURIOUS CUSTOMER. I'm going to come back here every day...

until I figure out who you are ;)

PATTY. what are you, a detective

CURIOUS CUSTOMER. That's exactly what I am.

8. I Didn't Know You Could Toast That

> (**LISA**'s first suggestion – almost against her
> will – but it's so good she can't resist –)

LISA. "I Didn't Know You Could Toast That."

> (Silence.)

Poor Man's Cookbook, Colon, I Didn't Know You Could
Toast That.

> (Silence.)

so it's all...

things...

you cook...

> (Waiting for her mom to chime in but she
> doesn't.)

...in a toaster.

> (Suspenseful pause here? Or straight to:)

GEORGINA. Jackpot.

LISA. seriously?

GEORGINA. Honey, jackpot.

LISA. no

GEORGINA. Poor Man's Cookbook: I Didn't Know You
Could Toast That!!!

LISA. "jackpot"?

GEORGINA. It's our first idea!

It's our first real real real idea!

And we made it together!

LISA. but name one recipe like Name One

GEORGINA. *(Duh.)* Poor man's pizza is toasted bread with mayonnaise and ketchup

LISA. that's disgusting.

GEORGINA. if you're actually destitute –

LISA. you don't have a toaster

you don't have mayonnaise

GEORGINA. I was gonna say you don't have pizza

LISA. you're not buying "little books by the cash register."

(Instant spin, damage control.)

GEORGINA. okay, so maybe

Poor Man's Cookbook

...is targeting bougie people...!

who are romanticizing poverty

(Abrupt pause as they think about that.)

9. Hurried Customer

HURRIED CUSTOMER. coffee coffee quick quick quick I'm
   late I'm late

PATTY. *(Zen, gnomic.)* ...it's not *my* fault

   ...that *you* are late

HURRIED CUSTOMER. Let's go, Let's go,

   Java Java Java –

   Bean juice – Jitter juice – Miracle juice – Youth juice –

   Wake me up

   Wake me up inside

   Make me feel ANYTHING

   Hurry it up back there

PATTY. *(Calm and sweet and wise.)* being slightly less late

   is not worth

   being rude to people.

HURRIED CUSTOMER. I'm a SURGEON

   (Into phone, running off [?])

   prep the electrodes, stat –

   we're gonna make three incisions, just below the skull –

   do not let her die on me –

10. Job Loss

(**GEORGINA**'s *head is down on the table?*
Groaning softly.)

LISA. ...mom?

(**GEORGINA** *is doing a version of the groan*
that **LISA** *did earlier.*)

GEORGINA. ughhghgghghghgghgh

LISA. ...shouldn't you be at work?

GEORGINA. no.

LISA. ...aren't you usually

At Work right now?

GEORGINA. what are you talking about.

LISA. Mom.

GEORGINA. I wanna go back to bed.

LISA. What's going on?

(*Beat.*)

GEORGINA. remember how

you're always encouraging me

to ask for a raise

LISA. you deserve a raise.

GEORGINA. I asked for a raise.

LISA. Good job! Finally!

I'm proud of you.

GEORGINA. and they fired me.

(*Beat.*)

LISA. you asked for a raise –

GEORGINA. yep.

LISA. – and they fired you?

GEORGINA. mhm.

LISA. because...of me?

GEORGINA. well,

LISA. can that even happen?

GEORGINA. I think they finally took a hard look at the numbers and were like uh oh

LISA. "uh oh"?

GEORGINA. what's her "value"

is she "adding" "value"

    (Beat.)

LISA. were you?

GEORGINA. *is anyone????????????*

    (Beat.)

LISA. so

what does

"not having a job" –

mean?

GEORGINA. well,

LISA. for us?

are we still gonna have – food?

GEORGINA. we.

are going to reflect.

and be grateful.

LISA. *(Panic.)* ...because my friends all got new phones

and I kinda need a new phone too if I want to be still
friends with them

GEORGINA. deep breaths.

LISA. mom are we homeless?

GEORGINA. it's not impossible

that in the near future

you and I will have to make

what are called "Lifestyle Adjustments"

11. Lisa's Friend Is A Customer

LISA'S FRIEND IS A CUSTOMER. Lisa? oh my god Lisa!

LISA. oh no.

GEORGINA. what?

LISA. hide me.

GEORGINA. what?

LISA'S FRIEND IS A CUSTOMER. oh my god Lisa!

LISA. hide me now.

GEORGINA & LISA'S FRIEND IS A CUSTOMER. Hide you from what?

LISA. I want to die.

LISA & LISA'S FRIEND IS A CUSTOMER. Hiiiii!

GEORGINA. Lisa, is this your classmate?????

LISA. *(Humiliated.)* ...this is my mom

LISA'S FRIEND IS A CUSTOMER. Lisa's Mom wow hi Mrs. Lisa's Mom

> (**LISA** *is trying to hide their business ideas with her body.*)

GEORGINA. this is too cute

how do you two know each other?

> (**LISA** *is embarrassed,* **LISA'S FRIEND** *is excited.*)

LISA & LISA'S FRIEND IS A CUSTOMER. social justice club.

GEORGINA. what?

LISA & LISA'S FRIEND IS A CUSTOMER. social justice club

GEORGINA. Lisa.

You did not tell me you're in *clubs*.

LISA. just one.

GEORGINA. here I was thinking my daughter had no friends.

now I find out she's in *clubs*

LISA. it's not real

GEORGINA. what is this "club," then? can I join?

LISA'S FRIEND IS A CUSTOMER. *("No.")* it's…Social Justice Club?

GEORGINA. (here I was hoping it was like a country club)

LISA'S FRIEND IS A CUSTOMER. or like a clurrrb

LISA. *(Pious course correction.)* we mostly talk about evil and how to stop it.

GEORGINA. fun!

> *(Awkward pause.)*

what have you come up with?

LISA'S FRIEND IS A CUSTOMER. lead with love.

LISA. kill all grown-ups

GEORGINA. neat.

LISA'S FRIEND IS A CUSTOMER. to be honest, we mostly just flirt

GEORGINA. you – what?

LISA'S FRIEND IS A CUSTOMER. So! What'r u gals upta?

GEORGINA. Starting a business.

LISA. stupid it's stupid I know.

we're not really starting a business I promise

LISA'S FRIEND IS A CUSTOMER. no no I gotchu.

I got three business myself.

LISA. …you do?

LISA'S FRIEND IS A CUSTOMER. duh, colleges love it

good for the ol' resume

GEORGINA. what's your businesses?

LISA'S FRIEND IS A CUSTOMER. first is mental health sweaters

we connect sustainable cashmere farmers

with gen z influencers who have overcome depression

GEORGINA. (why didn't we think of that?)

LISA'S FRIEND IS A CUSTOMER. so that's been immediately profitable, woohoo

plus they, they look really good.

LISA. so but – what do *you* do?

LISA'S FRIEND IS A CUSTOMER. Leadership.

LISA. when you say you "connect" farmers –

LISA'S FRIEND IS A CUSTOMER. Email.

GEORGINA. how much are sweaters?

LISA'S FRIEND IS A CUSTOMER. what's your guys' business?

> (**GEORGINA** *looks at* **LISA** *expectantly –* "*You Do It!*")

LISA. (*Trying to be cool.*) Little Books...by the Cash Register

> (*Pause. Humiliation?*)

> (*But they're kind of flirting? Cool kid stand off –*)

LISA'S FRIEND IS A CUSTOMER. which...cash register

LISA. the.

the.

LISA'S FRIEND IS A CUSTOMER. ...people shop online

...people hate reading

(Eyes clamped shut [?] praying this works –
GEORGINA *mouths along encouragingly [?])*

LISA. YOU'RE BY A CASH REGISTER. You're sad.

Your life lacks whimsy.

And what should be smiling up at you?

But a little book.

About anything. FRANCE.

Designed by a...mother daughter team.

LISA'S FRIEND IS A CUSTOMER. ...yeah?

LISA. ...yeah.

LISA'S FRIEND IS A CUSTOMER. ...what's the profit margin
on that?

LISA. it's...for bougie people

who are romanticizing poverty.

(Pause ?????????)

LISA'S FRIEND IS A CUSTOMER. oops, I'm off.

Lisa, see you later, wink.

you really need to get a new phone.

(Humiliation.)

*(***GEORGINA*** whistles as* **LISA'S FRIEND IS A**
CUSTOMER *exits.)*

LISA, we gotta start a business, Mom.

we gotta start a real real real ass business.

by the time I go to

Social Justice Country Clurb

12. Boss

*(Patty's **BOSS** is a customer: all business.)*

BOSS. Patty.

PATTY. Boss!

　Hi Boss "Hi Boss"

BOSS. I need to talk to you about something.

PATTY. *(Word vomit.)* Please give me a raise.

　Why haven't you ever given me a raise?

　I do everything. I do a good job.

　Is there something wrong with *me*?

　You should also give me health insurance and time off
　and a 401k! and a Subaru! and a family

　and in return, I'm happy to take on – more responsibilities?

　like maybe I could get involved in – get ready for it –
　management?

　Financial management? Fiscal? Just an idea just a
　crazy idea.

　I've been practicing and that all came out wrong, but

　I need money. It's emotional for me.

　Even a few dollars would make a meaningful difference
　in my life.

　Thank you so much I really appreciate it. Sorry

BOSS. ...there have been complaints about you on Yelp.

PATTY. ...Yelp?

BOSS. *(Reading from her phone.)* Yelp.

　Quote:

"Sad punk made me uncomfortable. Asked me what I 'do.' Could any question be more boring? Ask me what I love."

PATTY. huh. weird!

BOSS. Here's another.

Quote:

"Weekend girl refused to stamp my stamp card. FUCKING FUCK WHAT THE FUCK, FUCK."

That's in caps lock.

PATTY. that didn't happen.

that one didn't happen

BOSS. Quote.

"Really wanted the cool barista to like me. Instead, she pulled me deep into a twisted psychological battle. Now I'm crying in my cubicle."

PATTY. ...I'm trying my best.

do I get to write reviews of them?

BOSS. Quote. "Barista has a funny face. Too funny.

I'm going to come back every day until I figure out who she is."

PATTY. that's – terrifying –

BOSS. Last one. Quote. "Because coffee was given to me slowly, a woman died."

(*Pause.*)

how hard is it to be nice?

smile more or we'll ask you to leave.

(**BOSS** *is exiting.*)

PATTY. SO, about that RAISE –

BOSS. every single Yelp review has to be perfect from now on.

PATTY. that's impossible.

that's like a fairy tale task.

like weave straw into gold.

BOSS. yup.

PATTY. ...what do you do?

all day long? while I'm here?

what do *you do*?

BOSS. I volunteer at an orphanage.

13. DMV Re-take

(**LISA** *begins to really apply herself.*)

(*Sticky notes and "visual research" get hung up on the wall as ideas accumulate –*)

LISA. okay okay okay

what if we somehow

gave people the option

to pay, say, a little bit of money –

(*~Suspense~*)

promise you won't make fun of me.

GEORGINA. I'm proud of you.

Proud.

My little entrepreneur.

LISA. to get their driver's license photo retaken!

like even just a human photographer instead of the creepy machine

or even just they take four shots and you get to *choose*

GEORGINA. (*Stricken –*) *you* thought of that?

LISA. is it good?

GEORGINA. right now?

you thought of that right now?

LISA. it's stupid, I'm stupid.

I'm a teenager!

I've never done a business idea before

GEORGINA. Lisa.

Every. Single. Person.

Would do it.

LISA. aaah!

> (**GEORGINA** *writes "2. DMV re-take" on the big piece of paper –)*

GEORGINA. I'm actually jealous.

I find myself wrestling jealousy.

LISA. so that's what, five dollars times –

GEORGINA. ten dollars –

LISA. twenty!

GEORGINA. twenty dollars times –

LISA. how many people in the united states?

GEORGINA. ka-ching

LISA. *(Doing fast math on a napkin –)* carry the one...

GEORGINA. forget paying for college...

we could pay the national debt

> *(So happy – all their problems solved – tears of joy –)*

LISA. mom.

oh my god, mom

GEORGINA. *(Intense –)* Don't mention this to anyone.

Someone could steal our idea.

LISA. *(Suddenly guarded, seeds of suspicion and jealousy.)* my...idea.

My idea.

(Knife fight.)

(Suddenly we're in Succession.*)*

GEORGINA. 60:40.

LISA. 80:20

GEORGINA. *(Weird panic.) You never would have thought of it without me.*

LISA. 70:30 last offer

(Handshake.)

GEORGINA. atta girl

LISA. good game

GEORGINA. *(Uh-oh.)* we'd have to collaborate with the DMV.

14. Forward Customer

(**FORWARD CUSTOMER** *is nervous.*)

(**PATTY** *is trying to smile.*)

PATTY. smiling

I'm smiling

what can I get you :)

FORWARD CUSTOMER. *(Nervous, excited, pumping himself up for this.)* A Date.

PATTY. what

FORWARD CUSTOMER. sure you get this all the time, but:

I would like one date with you please.

(*Beat!*)

PATTY. ...why?

FORWARD CUSTOMER. why not

all the usual reasons

what do you mean "why"?

PATTY. why...

would you...

wanna date...

with me

FORWARD CUSTOMER. you're cute.

PATTY. *(Suspicious –)* I'm...at work.

FORWARD CUSTOMER. you're cute at work

PATTY. I'm sorry I just can't understand why anyone, um.

how anyone could, like.

have that reaction. to my situation.

> (**FORWARD CUSTUMOR** *takes-that-in pause.*)

FORWARD CUSTOMER. *(Judgmental.)* wow.

maybe we shouldn't go on a date.

PATTY. what do you do?

FORWARD CUSTOMER. what, do you only fuck finance boys ????????????

PATTY. I don't fuck

anyone

I'm just trying to imagine a different life for myself

FORWARD CUSTOMER. *(Sudden accent? Or accent the whole time.)* I'm the Duke of Windsor.

> *(Can that feel like the end of the scene?)*

PATTY. ...what

FORWARD CUSTOMER. I'm a customer service representative. Large coffee five Splendas

15. Easy Gender Swap

GEORGINA. skin care for men

LISA. that exists

GEORGINA. a masculine...brush

LISA. a comb?

GEORGINA. the idea is minimum work, maximum return
because the product's the same but the package is blue
so it's *doable,* do-able

LISA. salad – for men

GEORGINA. interesting, hey, interesting

LISA. salad for men?

(They get stuck in little loop.)

GEORGINA. salad for men

LISA. salad for men

GEORGINA. male salad

LISA. – or fruit? Masculine fruit?

GEORGINA. some kind of macho vegetable

LISA. potatoes? eggplant

GEORGINA. butch artichoke, killer romaine,

LISA. or feminized meat

GEORGINA. wow if we could somehow
feminize meat

LISA. and then charge ten percent more. and then retire early.

GEORGINA. is it pink?

LISA. rare, rare hamburger

GEORGINA. *(Just spitballing here.)* lip steak, hip steak, slim steak,

LISA. *(Worried.)* how do we *get* the food?

GEORGINA. girl steak, flirty beef,

LISA. do we know farmers?

GEORGINA. *("No.")* Lisa this is 101. Everyone everywhere has everything everywhere.

LISA. people have nothing

GEORGINA. so the battle becomes: branding. everyone "has" artichoke.

but only our artichoke. Means sex

16. Shy Customer

PATTY. Smiling smiling smiling.

What can I get you? :)

SHY CUSTOMER. do you know where everyone is getting the laptops?

PATTY. ...huh?

SHY CUSTOMER. everyone at every table has laptops?

where are they coming from?

PATTY. stores?

SHY CUSTOMER. is there like a laptop sign-out sheet?

PATTY. I think they...

brought them.

from their homes.

SHY CUSTOMER. I guess I hoped because the café has a sign that says

"our coffee empowers farmers in the global south"

and another sign that says

"our beans inspire teenaged girls to always be themselves no matter what"

there might be, like –

god I'm such an embarrassing idiot.

(Pause.)

PATTY. what do you do?

SHY CUSTOMER. I'm in eighth grade

17. Uber for Hugs

GEORGINA. Uber for hugs.

LISA. two bucks a hug? tip your hugger?

GEORGINA. someone's lonely – someone's desperate – boom they're hugging.

LISA. I mean an actual *hug*? is worth...is priceless

GEORGINA. Very very very very elite hugs. Hugs for billionaires

LISA. *(Gross.)* Do you get to choose who hugs you though?

GEORGINA. *(Pretending to be a lecherous old man scrolling the app –)* hell I need a hug. I need a hug right now.

LISA. hey I'm googling and – it already exists.

GEORGINA. what? but we thought of it first.

LISA. It exists.

GEORGINA. Uber for hugs? Exists? try Lyft for hugs.

LISA. it exists and there's already – yeah. multiple lawsuits

18. Heartbroken Customer

(**HEARTBROKEN CUSTOMER** *wears a bulky winter coat.*)

HEARTBROKEN CUSTOMER. my wife...is cheating on me.

PATTY. oh

HEARTBROKEN CUSTOMER. with like. three other dudes.

PATTY. three?

HEARTBROKEN CUSTOMER. maybe four. big dudes. big. five of them.

PATTY. do you...want coffee?

HEARTBROKEN CUSTOMER. I don't know what to do. I'm having violent fantasies.

PATTY. mmm.

HEARTBROKEN CUSTOMER. you get it. wow. you know how sometimes – with a stranger – you just – bam – connect?

PATTY. *(Trying it.)* I'm having a hard day too, actually –

HEARTBROKEN CUSTOMER. the crazy thing is – I still love her! I love her! I love that crazy girl.

hell I'm proud of her, I hope she's having fun.

PATTY. ...what do you do?

HEARTBROKEN CUSTOMER. I'm a youth pastor

19. All Ages Bar

(More and more sticky notes –)

GEORGINA. All Ages Bar.

LISA. it's...illegal?

GEORGINA. have a beer – bring your kid

LISA. it's illegal.

GEORGINA. but it's *All Ages Bar*

LISA. or – Add A Bar

GEORGINA. what's Add a Bar?

LISA. Add A Bar, Also A Bar

GEORGINA. *(Thinking about it.)* "Also A Bar"...

LISA. whatever you have, now it's

GEORGINA & LISA. Also a Bar

LISA. so who we are is:

we're the chicks who come in –

GEORGINA. we have uniforms?

LISA. and Add A Bar

GEORGINA. Add an All Ages Bar ?

LISA. Say you're a zoo – boom. Zoo Bar.

Say you're a – store? Boom. Bar store.

GEORGINA. there's already Zoo Bars.

LISA. Dentist Bar. Morgue Bar.

Build-A-Bar Workshop

GEORGINA. but I liked my All Ages angle

LISA. selling to kids though?

tequila to *toddlers*?

GEORGINA. I just liked it.

I liked it because I thought of it.

LISA. it's unhealthy –

it's bad parenting –

GEORGINA. it was a good phrase

LISA. corporate ethics are important to young consumers –

GEORGINA. what if – for every one drink sold – we donate a drink

to a person in need

20. Coddling Customer

(This **CUSTOMER** *is sixty-odd years old with
like three scarves and a tote bag.)*

*(She would kiss you on both cheeks, just like
Paris, if she only could.)*

CODDLING CUSTOMER. well aren't you

the most adorable thing

I've ever seen!

PATTY. ha

CODDLING CUSTOMER. in fact, you're so adorable...

you almost make me...

wanna die!

PATTY. so, we're actually

a business!

I'm at work right now

CODDLING CUSTOMER. don't you like chatting?

isn't this the stuff of life?

PATTY. please tell me quickly and clearly what you want
while making eye contact then say thank you once,
simply, as you pay and leave

CODDLING CUSTOMER. excuse me

when did *money*

become more important to you

than *friendship*?

Ebenezer Scrooge

PATTY. I have to refill the Splenda, rotate the milks,

CODDLING CUSTOMER. boo-hoo

PATTY. and take care of myself emotionally

CODDLING CUSTOMER. boo-hoo for you

PATTY. I'm a poor hero and everyone else is a rich villain.

CODDLING CUSTOMER. what if I'm a goddess disguised as a beggar?

PATTY. your words control my body.

when you order,

my body has to move.

CODDLING CUSTOMER. that's normal

PATTY. all day long I say hi to people and they respond "two coffees"

hello two coffees hello two coffees

CODDLING CUSTOMER. that's normal, yup

PATTY. then at the end of the interaction I am required to *thank* them

all day long I thank people for laboring on their behalf

CODDLING CUSTOMER. *(Full yoga teacher:)* when we suffer, do we crumble?

when we suffer, do we abandon our values?

or – do we perhaps – find ourselves?

PATTY. you've never suffered

CODDLING CUSTOMER. no you've never suffered

PATTY. no you've never suffered

CODDLING CUSTOMER. no you've never suffered

PATTY. no you've never suffered

(Back to normal.)

CODDLING CUSTOMER. I've never had a mocha. What's a mocha?

PATTY. chocolate coffee.

CODDLING CUSTOMER. could you make it sound more appealing?

I'm kidding, I'm teasing, that appeals! one chocolate coffee mocha please

PATTY. six dollars.

CODDLING CUSTOMER. *six* dollars? shame!

people are *starving.*

do I look like I'm in finance?

PATTY. *(Hopeful.)* are you?

CODDLING CUSTOMER. I'm a choreographer.

and a rascal

and a fool

21. DMV Again

*(**LISA** speaks while she types.)*

LISA. Dear-info@DMV.gov,

GEORGINA. this isn't gonna work.

LISA. it's our only good idea.

GEORGINA. not gonna work.

LISA. We-are-a-local-family-business-with-an-exciting-business-idea-for-you.

GEORGINA. put "mother daughter team"

LISA. We'll-tell-you-what-it-is-

GEORGINA. "mother daughter team"

LISA. if-and-only-if-you-sign-the-attached-NDA.

(Ding!)

(Instant reply.)

GEORGINA. they wrote back fast –

LISA. "Dear local family business,

GEORGINA. something's off

LISA. Would love to hear your idea. Signed NDA attached. Looking forward, The DMV."

GEORGINA. don't respond.

LISA. *(Typing –)* Dear The DMV,

GEORGINA. Don't Respond –

LISA. Idea is twenty dollars for photo retakes.

You're welcome, Lisa.

(Ding!)

(Instant reply.)

(They read it aloud together:)

GEORGINA & LISA. Dear Lisa,

My name is Mikey. I work at the DMV answering phones and emails. When I'm not here I'm at my other job at Foot Locker or my other other job at the other Foot Locker. Sure, it makes me sad sometimes but I do love my turtles plus I try to remember that sacrifice creates meaning plus there is dignity in helping people. Also TV. What is your daily life like? I'd love to meet in person to discuss more and see where this can go. Also how old are you? Please send a photo, or preferably two photos, front and back. I think your business idea is cool but I just work here. Thanks and best, Mikey

22. Angry Customer

PATTY. (smiling is good for you)

   (it's actually healthier to smile)

ANGRY CUSTOMER. what's your name?

PATTY. I –

   don't have to tell you that.

ANGRY CUSTOMER. no really, what's your name?

PATTY. I know you think asking my name is "nice" or makes you "good"

   but it's actually an invasion of privacy

   and only gives you more power over me than you already have.

ANGRY CUSTOMER. are you trying to kill my child.

PATTY. what?

ANGRY CUSTOMER. my child was choking. hagging.

   on a hunk – hunk – of mold

PATTY. ew

ANGRY CUSTOMER. Mold.

PATTY. yuck

ANGRY CUSTOMER. he just vomited in the bathroom

PATTY. is he okay?

ANGRY CUSTOMER. yes! because I Love him

PATTY. we're so sorry – I'll get the mop

ANGRY CUSTOMER. what's your name?

   (Beat.)

PATTY. if you complain about me I'll lose my job.

do you really think this scary but harmless two-minute episode

is worth destroying my entire life?

ANGRY CUSTOMER. Yes.

(Beat.)

PATTY. what do you do?

ANGRY CUSTOMER. I'm a philanthropist.

23. LinkedIn

(Exhausted, weary, humbled by Mikey – verge of defeat –)

GEORGINA. I have 412 connections on LinkedIn.

and my goal.

is to have 500 connections on LinkedIn.

by the end of the month.

LISA. goals goals goals

I hate goals

maybe goal culture *is the problem*

GEORGINA. so that's –

how many connections per day?

LISA. why are you so obsessed with LinkedIn, Mom

GEORGINA. *(Frustrated –)* I heard the way to get jobs is through your weak ties

not your strong ties, your weak ties

counter-intuitive

heard it on a podcast

so what can I say, I'm just out here trying to get me some weak ties.

or maybe I should weaken my strong ties?

LISA. *(Weirdly scared or threatened –)* I'm your only strong tie

you're not gonna weaken your tie with – with me, mom

GEORGINA. well, honey, if I got a job again

we wouldn't have to rely on starting some miracle business!

With Mikey at the DMV!

LISA. *(Punching back –)* you know how people get jobs?

getting drinks with their bosses.

playing sports with their boss's nephews.

being born cool.

I figured this out just by watching TV like a normal person.

having 500 LinkedIn connections isn't good networking, it's embarrassing

GEORGINA. *(Hurt.)* it's not embarrassing.

I wouldn't say it's "embarrassing"

LISA. it's embarrassing how much time you've poured into a pathetic website.

it makes it seem like you have nothing going on in your life.

and don't know how to use the internet.

> *(**GEORGINA** is very hurt by that.)*

GEORGINA. I'm just trying to brainstorm actionable steps

I could take towards changing my life for the better

and LinkedIn was one of my only actionable steps I could brainstorm

and now you're taking my one good step away.

> *(Repeating under her breath:)*

I'm just trying to brainstorm actionable steps

I could take towards changing my life for the better

and LinkedIn was one of my only actionable steps I could brainstorm

and now you're taking my one good step away.

(Dust settles.)

*(**LISA** is disturbed to see her mom like this and wants to apologize but doesn't know how –)*

LISA. ...mom? I'm sorry

I don't understand anything about how the world works.

I don't even understand how stores have the right amount of things in them.

I don't know why I'm being mean to you

GEORGINA. I guess I wasted my time I'm deleting my account

LISA. don't delete it!

GEORGINA. my daughter informs me it's embarrassing I'm deleting it.

LISA. don't delete it!

GEORGINA. I'm deleting it

LISA. don't delete it!

GEORGINA. too late

(Click.)

(Miserably.) the laptop is running out of battery.

metaphor for my life

LISA. ...how many hours did you spend on that?

*(**GEORGINA** plugs the laptop in –)*

(The outlet is all the way across the café –)

(The power cord dangles precariously, suspended taught in midair –)

24. Laptop-for-Forty-Five-Minutes-Only Table

PATTY. *(Humiliated she has to speak this petty pseudo-branded language:)* this is a laptop-for-forty-five-minutes-only table?

GEORGINA. ...what

PATTY. this is a,

"laptop-for-forty-five-minutes-only table."

GEORGINA. (who is she?)

LISA. (she works here.)

GEORGINA. what are you saying?

PATTY. You can only use a laptop at this table for forty-five minutes.

On weekdays.

GEORGINA. are you...gonna time us?

PATTY. you also. haven't. ordered anything

GEORGINA. you gonna time us, nerd?

PATTY. not order. not *order.*

I have to work on that, even in myself.

would you two ladies like to politely ask me for some coffees?

(Beat.)

GEORGINA. so,

we're actually having a small, just a like *small*

cash flow issue?

LISA. *(Trying to be cool.)* how much is coffee?

PATTY. four fifty.

GEORGINA. mmmm, I was afraid of something like that

LISA. (you don't have four dollars and fifty cents?)

GEORGINA. *(Summoning all her charm –)* I think my colleague –

LISA. daughter

GEORGINA. partner / and I were hoping –

LISA. she's my mom

GEORGINA. that this charming café you so diligently custodian

functioned almost like a public co-working space

(Suspicious –)

PATTY. what do you guys do?

GEORGINA. we're entrepreneurs.

LISA. early stages

GEORGINA. we're job creators, you're welcome.

PATTY. what do you entreprenu?

GEORGINA. cool shit

salad for men

PATTY. so you're like

real business people?

GEORGINA. sure

PATTY. so you're actually

in business?

GEORGINA. what about us is unconvincing?

PATTY. finally.

can I ask you some questions?

GEORGINA. shoot.

PATTY. *(Eyes clapped shut?, fists clenched?, trying to articulate something too big –)* where...does money... come from?

GEORGINA. excuse me?

LISA. the earth.

GEORGINA. the bank

LISA. *(Trying to be cool.)* the social contract

PATTY. who owns all these buildings? like, who owns every building?

do you ever think about that?

like why is there a random parking lot, and does someone "own" it, and who am I?

GEORGINA. no.

PATTY. is "fiduciary" a noun or an adjective?

why do people sometimes say "financial" and sometimes say "fiscal"?

GEORGINA. where are you learning these words

PATTY. *is there a difference between financial and fiscal??????????????*

is not knowing the difference what's holding me back?

GEORGINA. you're a barista.

PATTY. what jobs *Are There*?

how much money is normal to have?

LISA. it's normal to be destitute.

PATTY. what should I do with the wad of $1 bills I make in my tip jar and store in my sock drawer?

GEORGINA. yikes

PATTY. "Invest" ??????????

LISA. practice gratitude.

PATTY. I just feel very deeply that

something is in some deep way...wrong. With everything.

and some people know the secret

and I somehow have not been told the secret...that everyone else has been told.

LISA. ...beautiful

PATTY. *give me the real shit.*

do not dumb it down for me.

give me the real shit, give it to me now.

GEORGINA. woah

PATTY. Answer my questions. Or I'll kill you.

LISA. *(Under her breath, turning away.)* (that's really hot)

GEORGINA. *("Back off" –)* so, I'm here with my teenaged daughter? we're a family

PATTY. sorry. gosh I'm so sorry.

GEORGINA. are you an entrepreneur?

PATTY. no. haha no. I'm just a server.

LISA. never "just" !

PATTY. I can't figure out if "server" or "barista" is more degrading

GEORGINA. barista.

LISA. if you're thinking about life as a competition, you've already lost.

GEORGINA. because a server could plausibly work someplace nicer.

LISA. I bet you're the best barista

in the whole wide world!

PATTY. so, I'm actually. seeking other employment

GEORGINA. *(Sudden job interview mode.)* what skills do
you have.

PATTY. I'm smart and hardworking

GEORGINA. what *skills*

PATTY. ...chatting

GEORGINA. we're not hiring at this time.

LISA. *(A strategic bargain:)* if.

you let us remain seated

at this laptop-for-forty-five minutes-only table

even though we haven't "ordered anything"

...

we.

will consider your application

for a position at our company

should one open up.

PATTY. aaaaaaaaaaaaaaaaaaaaaaaare

you serious?

> *(**LISA** looks at **GEORGINA**.)*

GEORGINA. ...yes

PATTY. oh my gosh

GEORGINA. don't be weird

PATTY. I have to go deal with this line of customers –

I'm happy to fill out a 1099 or a W2 or or –

25. Curious Customer Returns

CURIOUS CUSTOMER. I know you!

I do know you!

PATTY. You don't know me.

CURIOUS CUSTOMER. Patty!

You're Patty!

Patty, from undergrad?

PATTY. ...maybe I used to be.

that Patty is dead now.

CURIOUS CUSTOMER. *(Doing an ancient college dance/chant.)* it's me, Jane!

remember: Jaaaaaa-aaaa-aaa-aaaaane?

PATTY. ...hi Jane.

CURIOUS CUSTOMER. I can't believe this! aaah! what are you up to!

PATTY. I. Drink a lot of beer and watch TV on my computer.

...

I actually – just got in on the ground floor of a hot new startup

CURIOUS CUSTOMER. that's great :) :) :) :) :)

PATTY. ...what do you do?

CURIOUS CUSTOMER. I have three beautiful children.

Can you believe it? A freak like me.

Wanna see pictures?

26. American Girl Dolls

(Getting back into it – revving up –)

GEORGINA. Business Ideas, Business Ideas, quick before she comes back

LISA. Um Um Um

GEORGINA. Think get rich quick, think cheat code. Don't think, stop thinking.

LISA. that's dangerous

GEORGINA. it's facebook's motto. just go, un-block

GEORGINA.	**LISA.**
go go go go go	I'm trying, I can't,

LISA. okay, okay, I have some shit I could sell?

GEORGINA. *(Interested.)* what, like. drugs?

LISA. no, like – my old American Girl Dolls?

GEORGINA. *(Horrified.)* honey! no!

LISA. I could sell them on the street.

GEORGINA. but all our memories –

LISA. we could maybe get two hundred dollars –

GEORGINA. that won't even pay for one textbook –

27. Georgina's Friend is a Customer

(Nerd in a wannabe corporate vest.)

GEORGINA'S FRIEND IS A CUSTOMER. Georgina?

GEORGINA. oh no

LISA. what?

GEORGINA. hide me

LISA. what?

GEORGINA'S FRIEND IS A CUSTOMER. Hey Georgiana!

GEORGINA. hide me now

LISA & GEORGINA'S FRIEND IS A CUSTOMER. hide you from what?

GEORGINA. I want to die.

GEORGINA & GEORGINA'S FRIEND IS A CUSTOMER. Hiiiiiiiiii

LISA. mom is this your...

sad work friend?

GEORGINA. this is my daughter.

GEORGINA'S FRIEND IS A CUSTOMER. Little Georgina wow Hey Little Georgina's daughter

I'm George. He/Him/His.

LISA. This is too cute. How do you know each other?

*(**GEORGINA**, with grief:)*

(Her friend, with fondness:)

GEORGINA & GEORGINA'S FRIEND IS A CUSTOMER. Office softball club.

LISA. excuse me?

GEORGINA & GEORGINA'S FRIEND IS A CUSTOMER. Office softball club.

LISA. Mom

you did not tell me you're in *clubs*

GEORGINA'S FRIEND IS A CUSTOMER.   your mom's a slugger

LISA. here I thought mom had no friends

now I find out she's in *clubs*

(Absurd litany of office tropes:)

GEORGINA'S FRIEND IS A CUSTOMER. Hey, are we on the same slack channel?

You see that quarterly report?

Bloodbath. Bloodbath.

Oh my god, were you cc'd on that email?

Oh my god, were you *bcc'd*?

You sly devil, you were bcc'd, weren't you.

I never see you by the water cooler anymore.

*(**GEORGINA** and this man have obviously smooched.)*

LISA. are you...my dad?

GEORGINA. George.

GEORGINA'S FRIEND IS A CUSTOMER. Georgina.

GEORGINA. what's your salary?

GEORGINA'S FRIEND IS A CUSTOMER. uhh

woah there cowgirl

GEORGINA. how much do they pay you?

GEORGINA'S FRIEND IS A CUSTOMER. that's not the kinda thing –

GEORGINA. because we started at the same time, right?

GEORGINA'S FRIEND IS A CUSTOMER. vaguely –

GEORGINA. we had similar titles?

GEORGINA'S FRIEND IS A CUSTOMER. I mean you're more "associate" level –

GEORGINA. we were both associates.

GEORGINA'S FRIEND IS A CUSTOMER. "were"?

GEORGINA. disclose your entire financial situation to me right now.

GEORGINA'S FRIEND IS A CUSTOMER. did you get promoted?

I'm not jealous. I'm not jealous.

I'm proud of you. Equity.

LISA. *(Injustice.)* Mom got fired.

(**GEORGINA** *hits* **LISA** *[gently]*)

GEORGINA'S FRIEND IS A CUSTOMER. *(Surprise –)* oh shit

(Realizing he won –) damnnnn

(Realizing he's in trouble –) fuck

(Back to them, saving face.) ay carumba

(That was weird –) jeez louise

(This has gone on too long –) holy mackerel

LISA. we're here starting a business.

GEORGINA. stupid it's stupid I know

we're not really starting a business I promise

GEORGINA'S FRIEND IS A CUSTOMER. no no I gotchu

what's your guys's business?

(**LISA** *hits* **GEORGINA** *[gently]* like "Do It!")

GEORGINA. *(Very sadly [?] –)* American...Girl Dolls.

GEORGINA'S FRIEND IS A CUSTOMER. that's. pretty sure that one's already taken

GEORGINA. with drugs.

inside the American Girl Dolls.

American Girl Dolls filled with drugs.

GEORGINA'S FRIEND IS A CUSTOMER. ...like, penicillin?

GEORGINA. cocaine.

GEORGINA'S FRIEND IS A CUSTOMER. ...who's the target audience?

GEORGINA. shoppers.

> *(Pause.)*

so Kirstin's still out on the prairie

teaching kids about hard work and family

except this time she's filled. head to toe. with top shelf blow.

GEORGINA'S FRIEND IS A CUSTOMER. *(Honest.)* they always gave me 150k for just sitting around.

but last week – outta nowhere – they bumped me up to 200.

28. Struggling Customer

(**STRUGGLING CUSTOMER** *is unhoused and should probably be played very simply.*)

STRUGGLING CUSTOMER. ...

...

...

bathroom?

PATTY. oh gosh.

STRUGGLING CUSTOMER. ...

...

...

bathroom?

PATTY. *(Steely wall of performed professionalism.)* I'm afraid bathrooms are for customers only.

STRUGGLING CUSTOMER. ...

...

...

please?

PATTY. bathrooms are for customers only.

STRUGGLING CUSTOMER. ...

...

...

why?

(*Pause – it's a good question.*)

why not me?

PATTY. do you want coffee?

STRUGGLING CUSTOMER. no money

PATTY. here you can have one, you can have one for free if you leave.

STRUGGLING CUSTOMER. I'll have nowhere to pee it out

PATTY. if you go in the bathroom and poop everywhere, like last time –

STRUGGLING CUSTOMER. I won't do that

PATTY. or lock the door and sleep for twelve hours –

STRUGGLING CUSTOMER. I just want to clean my body

PATTY. I have to mop everything up. I can't do it again.

I'm sorry.

I'm not a bad person.

I'm only paid a little bit.

(Maybe this feels a little scary:)

STRUGGLING CUSTOMER. ...you're Patty, right?

...you take the bus here. The blue bus.

...do you have a bathroom where you live?

...what's your social security number?

PATTY. I have to ask you to leave.

you're disturbing the other patrons I have to ask you to leave.

STRUGGLING CUSTOMER. *(Genuinely sweet.)* I like talking with you, Patty.

thanks for always talking with me.

see you tomorrow.

have a blessed day.

PATTY. *(Blurting out –)* what do you do?

sorry, stupid.

how do you think about what you do in this life?

STRUGGLING CUSTOMER. I just try to help my friends out when I can

29. Gun App

*(**LISA** watched the above scene.)*

LISA. what if an invention could evaluate a power dynamic in a given room and if the power dynamic has injustice, this machine could like restore...justice

GEORGINA. so...a gun

LISA. the opposite of a gun

GEORGINA. a gun *app*

LISA. an app that kills people?

GEORGINA. if you could shoot people *from your phone*

LISA. that's terrifying

GEORGINA. we'd make so much money.

LISA. that's terrifying, mom.

you don't go to high school.

GEORGINA. if we don't do it.

someone else will.

(A moment of solemn purpose.)

(They ramp up into a flurry of eViL ideas:)

gun – car

LISA. tank

GEORGINA. tank phone

LISA. tank *purse*

GEORGINA. purse gun?

LISA. purse gun app. car

GEORGINA. good

LISA. for high schoolers.

GEORGINA. and it's cute.

LISA. *(New topic.)* Medicine.

GEORGINA. medicine, WHAT

LISA. something evil with medicine

GEORGINA. medicine, but fucked

LISA. a medicine that only makes you a little bit better

GEORGINA. and it's expensive. and it's addictive.

LISA. a medicine that keeps you sick.

GEORGINA. Nursing Homes

LISA. it looks like a nursing home...but there's no nurses... and it's not a home.

GEORGINA. it's just a big room with fluorescent lights in a strip mall

LISA. full of grandpas.

GEORGINA & LISA. pack 'em in tight.

GEORGINA. we put on one VHS – I dunno, *Shrek* –

LISA. *Finding Nemo*

GEORGINA. and let it play on repeat. forever.

GEORGINA & LISA. that's your nurse.

LISA. what if somehow – people pay us – large sums – every month – to live in the buildings – where *they* live.

GEORGINA. and if anyone needs help, like with a faucet or a doorknob, we don't respond.

LISA. *(Unhinged warlord –)* nine billion bucks for one drop of water! ten gazillion for one thin blanket!

GEORGINA. *(Disturbed – normalizing –)* we stand on the street and wipe people's windshields and hope people give us a dollar

30. Boss Returns

BOSS. Patty.

PATTY. Boss hi!

Hi Boss "Hi Boss"

BOSS. There are new Yelp reviews.

PATTY. sorry so sorry I'm sorry –

> (**BOSS** *reads these very skeptically and dryly.*)
>
> (*She has already read them – she is not discovering them –*)
>
> (*Each one makes her angrier than the last – so she gradually speeds up –*)

BOSS. Quote:

"the person behind the counter –

PATTY. I can do better I promise

BOSS. ...is the most beautiful person I've ever met in my entire life."

PATTY. ...me?

BOSS. "After months of torture, I finally worked up the courage to ask her out

And she let me down in the most graceful possible way."

Who is this guy?

PATTY. ...The Duke of Windsor

BOSS. Here's another. Quote.

"Nice lady helped me understand where laptops *come from*. Now I have an A in social studies."

PATTY. aw

BOSS. Quote. "Love is patient, love is kind. It does not boast, it is not proud. First Corinthians 13:4."

PATTY. he's a youth pastor

BOSS. Quote. "While I did not purchase a chocolate coffee mocha, I was invited into a new way of seeing. Patty behind the counter is a social worker, a community pillar, and a poet."

PATTY. ...a community pillar?

BOSS. Quote. "My child vomited on a hunk – hunk – of mold, but after a lot of genuflecting, I understand that accidents happen, especially in situations where workers are rushed and not properly respected or compensated, while in charge of complex food systems."

PATTY. wow

BOSS. Quote. "Omg Patty great to reconnect you little freak xoxo Jaaaaaaaaaaaaane"

PATTY. hi Jane

BOSS. Last one. Quote. "Patty I'm really sorry you had to clean up the bathroom after me, that makes me feel bad, I didn't know where else to go. I'm in the library now using the computer."

     (**PATTY** *is quietly moved.*)

PATTY. ...so

have I been smiling enough?

BOSS. *(Finally breaking/flipping.)* I have no one in my life.

I feel...jealous of you.

PATTY. don't the – little kids love you?

BOSS. what little kids?

PATTY. at the – orphanage?

BOSS. It's not a real orphanage. It's a video game.

It's a video game I'm addicted to where you play an elf who's volunteering at an orphanage.

It's an elf orphanage.

> *(–* **PATTY** *does not to respond to that –)*

Look I'll be honest with you Patty.

This place has yet to turn a profit.

I'm sinking cash into it.

It's basically a passion project at this point.

I always wanted to have a little café.

I can't give you a raise. That's it.

PATTY. *(Like a cartoon rabbit –)* iiiiiiiiiiiii quit!

BOSS. excuse me

> *(Does she do something silly like throw the wooden stir sticks everywhere? And then clean them up immediately after?)*

PATTY. as it so happens – this very morning – I got in on the ground floor –

of a hot new startup !!!!!!!!

BOSS. *(Interested.)* what's the startup?

PATTY. iiiiiiiii QUIT!!!

motherfucker

BOSS. *(Mumbling?)* because I'm actually – seeking other employment

> *(***LISA** *cannot stomach this.)*

LISA. there's been a horrible misunderstanding.

PATTY. There has? No there hasn't

LISA. We're not business people.

We're not in business.

We're out of business.

She got fired from Starbucks corporate last week when she asked for a raise.

I'm a B student in high school.

We're brainstorming business ideas to pay for college.

PATTY. *(Heart is breaking.)* oh.

GEORGINA. but the thought that we "could" "get rich" "at any moment"...tortures me

PATTY. oh.

(**BOSS** *is back to normal as they exit –)*

BOSS. I'm gonna start confiscating your tips, FYI. Standard practice.

PATTY. oh. kay

LISA. ...if it makes you feel any better. I'm in love with you.

(**LISA** *goes in for a kiss ??????????????????)*

PATTY. *(Ignoring that – rock bottom:)* I'm eighty thousand dollars in student debt.

LISA & GEORGINA. *(Fascinated, hungry.)* you are?

GEORGINA. what did you study?

PATTY. I have a PhD in sociology.

GEORGINA. gee

PATTY. my dissertation was titled

"Myth-Making and Dissonance, Colon

Performative Interventions and Hybrid Life Outcomes in Three Micro-Cultures"

LISA. *(Magical, self involved.)* wow it's almost like –

we're in a time loop –

and I *become* you

31. Meet Ruth

(Meet **RUTH**, *a mild-mannered good-natured customer –)*

RUTH. excuse me –

PATTY. FUCK OFF.

go FUCK YOURSELF

RUTH. oh

my god

PATTY. Sorry. Wow so sorry

I'm having a hard day.

RUTH. I find – when I'm a little nicer –

the world is nicer back

PATTY. or maybe if I got even meaner – like if I could only get mean enough –

everyone else would realize they're fucked up

RUTH. you can't control your circumstances

but you can control how you react to them

PATTY. I can't even control that.

...

would you like a free coffee?

RUTH. thank you.

that's very kind.

PATTY. what do you do?

RUTH. I was actually going to ask...if you're hiring?

32. Lisa Quits

GEORGINA. You know what?

I think a chain of cheap nursing homes…

I think that would work

LISA. Mom?

GEORGINA. maybe it seems "cruel" but it's not cruel to offer services to people on a budget –

LISA. I don't wanna do business ideas anymore.

GEORGINA. …you don't "want" to?

LISA. I never wanna do business ideas again.

GEORGINA. But, honey –

I'm having so much fun doing this with you this morning.

I'm having the time of my life.

> (**LISA** *starts taking their papers down.*)

LISA. we're never gonna do these.

we're never gonna do any of these anyway.

GEORGINA. stop! what are you doing?

LISA. they're not real.

they're just your embarrassing hobby

GEORGINA. *(Trying to hang them back up.)* but but but but but but – I love them!

I felt creative

> (**LISA** *rips more papers down –* **GEORGINA** *fights to keep them up – long messy scene:)*

LISA. I am so ashamed –

to be sitting here scheming –

LISA. while we watch those two women bend over to scrub coffee stains off the floor.

GEORGINA. Let that motivate you!

Think "I don't want to be them!"

LISA. they must hate us.

GEORGINA. they seem fine.

LISA. ...should we hate ourselves?

GEORGINA. that won't help anyone.

LISA. *(Demanding.)* should we or should we not hate ourselves.

GEORGINA. already do, ha.

>   (**LISA** *stops taking ideas down for a moment –)*

LISA. *(Measured, trying to articulate it.)* mom the other day you said

"we're not working class"?

and you said it with pride?

which is something I might say

...with shame.

GEORGINA. Honey. forget "working class," "not working class" –

you don't work.

LISA. relationships are work.

GEORGINA. relationships are work my ass

LISA. *(A thesis statement.)* I don't want to be an entrepreneur, Mom.

I'd rather be a worker.

GEORGINA. ...but Lisa

you need things, normal things, in your life, like

A Kitchen. A Subaru

LISA. those aren't normal

GEORGINA. Days Off, Two Babies

LISA. those are unconscionable luxuries.

GEORGINA. a new phone, don't you need a new phone?

LISA. look at our fucked-up ideas –

"Gun app"? "All Ages Bar"?

what's the point of going to college if not to learn stuff like this is wrong?

GEORGINA. no one can afford college without "stuff like this."

LISA. *(Clear-eyed.)* I don't want to be an entrepreneur, Mom.

I'd rather be a worker.

GEORGINA. ...who are you?

...where did you come from?

...did I make you?

...how could I have made you?

(Grandiose manifesto: standing on a table? Or something stupider:)

LISA. I reject all conventional notions of success!

Failure and only failure does not offend me!

GEORGINA. okay your highness,

okay you idiot,

okay you total punk rock rebel who I am not cool enough to hang out with,

LISA. as long as someone somewhere makes thirty cents a day –

I want to be with that person!

GEORGINA. and do what, hug them?

LISA. YES

GEORGINA. You say that, but you don't. You don't.

because first of all, the smell

LISA. even if our personal lives get better:

other people's lives will still be shit.

even if we somehow achieve our embarrassing, narcissistic goals:

other people will still be stuck in deep deep holes

GEORGINA. honey I fear you're conflating some very interesting political thoughts...

with just basic mental health

LISA. why do I...have to go to college.

GEORGINA. I don't understand the question.

LISA. you can't force me to go deep into debt just to get alcohol poisoning at some B student shithole –

GEORGINA. I would rather.

Die in a ditch.

Than see my only daughter uneducated.

> (**LISA** *is serious and vicious but I think this line is funny – genre trope –*)

LISA. I'm awake. For the first time in my life. I'm awake.

And you're asleep.

GEORGINA. *(Dire, threatening.)* imagine a future.

in which you cannot afford any café like this

all the friends you think you have now are in a totally differently socio-economic playing field

LISA. but you'll still hang out with me.

GEORGINA. you live in some shitty rat-infested group home.

you're not young and cute anymore. You are a burden.

LISA. you'll still hang out with me though, right?

GEORGINA. *In This Scenario I'm Dead.*

I am actually just desperately trying to impress upon you that I don't have time for your altruistic theatrics because I am terrified every day about the future.

LISA. *(Quiet? – Calmer –? –)* the amount of money you have

is a measure of how violent you are.

GEORGINA. Honey.

You drink twelve dollar green juices.

LISA. Everything we have is made possible by abused bodies.

GEORGINA. ...I almost want to say "duh"

LISA. So so so so what so.

So you're just LIVING WITH THAT?

GEORGINA. Baby I don't know what else to do.

...

There has to be some space between:

"Bullies win, winner takes all, power is the only truth."

And

"I deserve nothing, I eat crumbs, having anything is evil."

GEORGINA. ...

And we have to carve out that middle space. And that's the space we have to live in.

>   *(Beat.)*

LISA. I feel intense shame mom.

I don't know how else to describe it.

I feel an intense fiery shame all over my body.

GEORGINA. ...should we go see a doctor?

LISA. I don't want to do Business Ideas anymore.

GEORGINA. honey

>   *(Ultimate tactic: Begging? Or something else.
>   Dignity? Or just explaining.)*

in every bedtime story

my mother ever read

the princess always starts

her own business at the end.

LISA. I resign as Co-Founder and co-CEO of Mother-Daughter Start-Up LLC.

33. Patty Trains Ruth

(Our actor plays **RUTH** *and* **NICE CUSTOMER** *at once [!] Magic moment.)*

RUTH. good morning!

what can I get you?

NICE CUSTOMER. one coffee please!

aren't you gonna ask me what I do?

RUTH. huh?

NICE CUSTOMER. the other counter person always asks me what I do.

she's asked me what I do like eight times and it hasn't changed.

I'm still attorney general

RUTH. Neat!

NICE CUSTOMER. Okay! Have a good day, you.

RUTH. I *will*.

> *(***NICE CUSTOMER*** is gone. ***RUTH*** waves bye-bye.)*

> *(***PATTY*** is shocked and enraged ***RUTH*** had a nice interaction and speaks very quietly.)*

PATTY. ...how

RUTH. what's that?

PATTY. how

RUTH. how what

PATTY. how...will you have...

a good day?

RUTH. we're healthy

we're safe

we're indoors

we have faces

and relationships

> (**RUTH** *cleans something.*)

> (**PATTY** *stares at her feet.*)

why, do people tip more if we seem miserable?

> (*Still staring at her feet – or similar –*)

PATTY. I, like.

don't, like.

anything.

about my daily experience.

RUTH. oh

oh no

PATTY. and I can't figure out if it's *normal* to be this sad, or.

...welcome to your first day of work

RUTH. ...how's your social life?

do you ever read novels?

PATTY. (*Finally letting it out.*) conditions here are awful

how do you not see that?

beep beep beep beep dungeon

literally I never dreamed life could be so horrible and narrow –

RUTH. (*A healing mantra.*) no type of work.

is better or worse.

than any other type of work.

PATTY. what

RUTH. no type of work.

is better or worse.

than any other type of work.

PATTY. what the fuck

RUTH. if you're thinking about life as a competition you've already lost.

PATTY. I wish I could be like "fuck it I'm a badass working chick" –

but I'm not just ashamed of having this shit job,

I'm ashamed *that I'm ashamed* of having this shit job

RUTH. it's not a shit job

PATTY. I'm losing my personality.

I don't have a personality anymore.

RUTH. I like that it's social, I like being in my body, I like feeding people, I like working as a team,

PATTY. I feel like everyone else gets to be this happy idiot

who says whatever they want whenever they want lalala

while I've become this bitter shadow dweller

who only ever gets to say "that'll be four dollars, thank you for treating me like shit –"

RUTH. did you know

every attempt to unionize restaurant workers in New York City has failed?

because none of them identify as restaurant workers.

they all think they're about to become something else

PATTY. what are you talking about?

RUTH. *it's not bad to be in food service!*

I feel like you're talking a little like it's like bad to be in food service, or something

and frankly – that really offends me.

PATTY. *(Trying to convince her.)* I steal toilet paper, paper towels, bread, and coffee from this place to make rent.

RUTH. should you...be fired?

PATTY. I think I broke my finger but I'm afraid of going to the doctor.

I have bedbugs for the fifth time.

RUTH. at least you have a bed

PATTY. what is wrong with you?

you're like some brainwashed baby

feel sorry for me

RUTH. this is way better than my last job –

PATTY. *(Unhinged? Baby?)* feel SORRY FOR ME

> *(Pause.)*

RUTH. Besides working here...

Is there anything you do do? In your life? What do you do?

PATTY. ...LinkedIn

RUTH. what's that?

PATTY. LinkedIn.

RUTH. I can't hear what you're saying

PATTY. *(Intense shame.)* LinkedIn.

I have a LinkedIn. LinkedIn

I've been adding customers on LinkedIn.

that's why I always ask them what they do so I can find them and add them.

because I heard the way to get jobs is through "networking" which.

I don't even understand what that is or how to do it

and I don't have anyone else to network with!

but it's just hard because I hate every customer so much.

and they're all eighth graders and therapists anyway so it doesn't even work.

> *(Dust settles.)*

RUTH. *(Gently.)* I say this from a place of love

PATTY. don't say it

RUTH. you're embarrassing yourself.

LinkedIn is for old moms.

PATTY. no, no. it's for professionals

RUTH. you'd have more luck on the snapchat

PATTY. I was just trying to brainstorm actionable steps I could take.

towards changing my life for the better.

and LinkedIn was one of my only actionable steps I could brainstorm.

and now you're taking my one good step away.

> *(Silence.)*

I was just trying to brainstorm actionable steps I could take.

towards changing my life for the better.

PATTY. and LinkedIn was one of my only actionable steps I could brainstorm.

and now you're taking my one good step away.

RUTH. Patty? I'm sorry

I just met you and

it seems like you do a really good job keeping the napkins refilled

and keeping the wooden stir sticks refilled, too

PATTY. I'm deleting my LinkedIn.

RUTH. what? no

PATTY. my coworker informs me it's embarrassing I'm deleting it.

RUTH. don't delete it!

PATTY. I'm deleting it

RUTH. don't delete it!

PATTY. too late

(*Click.*)

RUTH. I'm sorry Patty.

it seems like you're having a. disappointing life.

PATTY. thank you.

that's all I wanted anyone to say.

RUTH. disappointing in a way so mild.

it's hard to even complain about

34. Career Quiz

*(**GEORGINA**, exhausted, war veteran, unplugs the laptop. They're leaving –)*

GEORGINA. we're gonna do a career quiz. so it's gonna say a career.

and you're gonna respond Like, Dislike, or Neutral.

ready?

LISA. neutral.

GEORGINA. would you like to:

keep records of payments received.

LISA. ...neutral.

GEORGINA. verify quality of parts before shipment.

LISA. neutral.

GEORGINA. examine artifacts left behind by previous civilizations.

LISA. neutral.

GEORGINA. apologize to your mother.

and accept your mother's apology.

and go home.

and take out, like, a lot of student loans.

and study something cool. like bugs. and how bugs live.

LISA. ...neutral.

GEORGINA. install drywall in houses

35. Ruth's Last Job

>*(Alone,* **PATTY** *and* **RUTH** *clean up the mess* **GEORGINA** *and* **LISA** *left behind.)*

PATTY. it's 6:05 a.m.

only five minutes have passed this whole time.

RUTH. huh.

...time flies!

PATTY. there's nine hours left in our shift.

>*(Pause. They drink coffee? First real coffee in the play?)*

what was your last job?

RUTH. *(Mildly.)* what's that?

PATTY. you said this was way nicer than your last job.

what do you do?

RUTH. ...I

worked in a canning factory for fifteen years.

Until I was fired – last winter – when my fingers got so calloused I couldn't bend them anymore.

I took a job as a truck driver. I drove through the night on no sleep delivering Amazon boxes.

Until last week I was so tired I ran over a family's dog.

I took a job in a coal mine. I died in that coal mine. But I came back as a model.

I wasn't allowed to eat, I cried all the time I was so hungry. Until I was fired when I turned nineteen.

I signed up for what I thought was a temporary gig as a homemaker that lasted five thousand years.

I had to clean up my husband's vomit and edit his manuscripts.

I lived in a tent in a Walmart parking lot and survived on frozen waffles.

I built iPhone chips with my bare hands in a sweatshop with no air conditioning.

I've been drafted, I was a frontline soldier in a meaningless war

and I died fighting for a cause I didn't believe in. That actually happened a lot of times.

and I change diapers. and I farm potatoes. and I build skyscrapers.

so, yeah. but that's just what I do.

End

www.ingramcontent.com/pod-product-compliance
Lightning Source LLC
Chambersburg PA
CBHW070635120726
47909CB00004B/1441